THE
Missing Mongoose

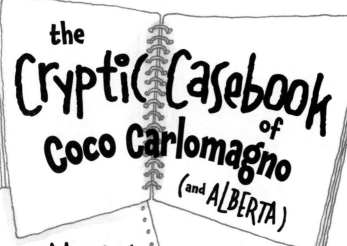

the Cryptic Casebook of Coco Carlomagno (and ALBERTA)

THE Missing Mongoose

URSULA DUBOSARSKY

ILLUSTRATIONS BY
TERRY DENTON

ALLEN&UNWIN
SYDNEY·MELBOURNE·AUCKLAND·LONDON

First published in 2013
Copyright © Text, Ursula Dubosarsky 2013
Copyright © Illustrations, Terry Denton 2013

Allen & Unwin
83 Alexander Street
Crows Nest NSW 2065
Australia
Phone: (61 2) 8425 0100
Email: info@allenandunwin.com
Web: www.allenandunwin.com

A Cataloguing-in-Publication entry is available from the
National Library of Australia – www.trove.nla.gov.au

ISBN 978 174331 260 5

Coco's favourite tango is 'Mi Buenos Aires Querido'
(My Beloved Buenos Aires), 1934; music by Carlos Gardel,
lyrics by Alfredo Le Pera, translation by Joseph del Genio
Cover and text design by Liz Seymour
Set in 16/21 pt Adobe Jenson Pro
This book was printed in May 2013 at McPherson's Printing Group,
76 Nelson Street, Maryborough, Victoria 3465, Australia.
www.mcphersonsprinting.com.au

10 9 8 7 6 5 4 3 2 1

To Anna, the inspirational!
– Ursula

Note to reader: If there is a word in the story you haven't seen before, it may be in Spanish, the language of Argentina. Have a look in the glossary at the back to find out what it means.

Chapter One

Alberta was perched on top of a ladder in the living room, hanging a picture on the wall, when she felt a letter poking out from under the picture frame.

'Ah,' she said to herself. 'I bet that's from Coco.'

Coco was Alberta's cousin. He was Chief of Police in Buenos Aires, a big city in South

America. Alberta had been expecting to hear from him. It was about time for another emergency.

She climbed carefully from the ladder and sat down to read the letter. This is what it said:

Dear Alberta,

Something so dreadful is going on here, I cannot it any longer.

Please come and help me—
I'm despe e!

BTW, the weather is breezy, so don't forget your rdigan.

kisses and hugs,
your devoted cousin,
Coco.

2

Alberta read the letter through twice, while her enormous brain wondered.

'I think,' she decided at last, 'that I will hang the picture another day. I'd better get over there, on the double!'

She folded up the ladder, and packed some lettuce leaves and a game of chequers in a brown-paper bag – and a cardigan, just in case.

Then she left a note for the piano tuner, locked the door behind her and headed off for South America.

Chapter Two

By the time Alberta arrived in Buenos Aires, the sun was blazing high in the sky. She made an urgent stop at her favourite fruit-salad stall and ate a lovely plate of frozen strawberries.

Feeling refreshed, she headed for Coco's office at the top of the Obelisco, the tallest monument in the city. After climbing all 206 steps she was quite pink with heat again. How glad she was to see the familiar door with its splendid shiny sign!

'Alberta! You're here at last!'

Before she could knock, the door opened wide and there stood Coco, looking as if he was just about to go out. He kissed Alberta on both her furry cheeks, which is the custom in South America.

'I came as soon as I received your letter, Coco,' said Alberta.

'I am so glad you did, Alberta,' replied Coco. 'I'm desperate for your help. A dreadful calamity has befallen the city – perhaps the most dreadful in all its history!'

'I am sorry to hear that,' said Alberta calmly. 'What is it?'

'You cannot imagine.' Coco clutched at his heart. 'Something so terrible, so horrible—'

'Is it to do with animals?' interrupted Alberta, thinking of the letter.

'Alberta, that brain of yours!' Coco gazed at her in admiration. 'I don't know how you do it. It *is* to do with animals. In particular, the wonderful Buenos Aires Zoo. And it's so ghastly, so horrifying—'

He sank down on his knees and his voice dropped to a gurgling whisper.

'One of their mongooses is missing!'

Alberta blinked.

'Goodness!' she said. 'That is – er – unexpected. But I wonder, Coco, shouldn't that be "mongeese"? "Mongooses" doesn't sound quite right.'

'I don't know, Alberta,' said Coco, shaking his head sadly. 'At the moment, all I know is that their most prized mongoose is missing. We must go to the Zoo right away!'

'Yes, of course,' agreed Alberta. 'Will we take your scooter?'

'Alas, my scooter is in the repair shop,' confessed Coco. 'I accidentally left an empanada in the motor, and it started making a strange noise. So we will have to take the bus. But not to worry! The buses in Buenos Aires are the wonder of the world. Vamos!'

The cousins scampered down the 206 steps and out onto the huge roundabout

that surrounded the Obelisco. It took rather a long time to cross the road to the bus stop, as there were many lanes of traffic and not every driver was expert at spotting two small pedestrian guinea pigs.

But finally they reached the other side and looked up at all the signs with numbers displayed for all the different buses.

'Great carrots! There are so many to choose from!' said Alberta. 'Which one do we take, primo?'

'A ver,' said Coco, 'according to the Zookeeper, we need to take four different buses. She said it doesn't actually matter which ones, as long as all the numbers add up to two hundred and seventy-three.'

'That is a very strange system,' said Alberta. 'If I may say so.'

'Perhaps,' said Coco. 'But I can assure you, everyone always arrives at the right destination.'

CAN YOU WORK OUT
A COMBINATION OF BUSES
COCO AND ALBERTA COULD TAKE?
THERE MAY BE MORE THAN
ONE RIGHT ANSWER!

Look at the back of the book for some tips to help you work it out.

Chapter Three

Coco and Alberta managed to find four buses for the legendary Buenos Aires Zoo. The only problem was that all the stops and starts and curves and turns gave Coco terrible travel sickness.

'I can't wait till my scooter is fixed,' he said to Alberta as he staggered off the last bus in front of the Zoo. 'I am not strong enough for that much excitement.'

On the high silver gates was a large sign that read:

The Zookeeper, a striking beauty with multicoloured fur, rushed out of the gates to greet them.

'Señor Coco! I am so glad to see you!'

'Dear Señorita Zookeeper,' said Coco, putting on his most handsome face. 'Never fear! I am here now!'

'So am I,' mentioned Alberta.

'Yes, this is my cousin Alberta,' introduced Coco. 'She is a genius at solving mysteries.'

'Is that so?' said the Zookeeper.

'And Alberta, this is the Zookeeper,' continued Coco. 'She is a specialist in mongooses. She's always being interviewed about them on television.'

'That is quite amazing,' commented Alberta.

'Please come in,' said the Zookeeper, ushering them through the gates. 'As you see, we have closed the Zoo to the public on account of the catastrophe.'

They followed the Zookeeper inside. It was clear that all the animals were upset: there was the sound of mournful sobbing from every species.

'Let's sit down here,' said the Zookeeper, pointing to a bench next to a pond of bright blue water filled with weeping fairy penguins. 'I will tell you all about it.'

Luckily the fairy penguins did most of their crying underwater, so it was not too noisy for conversation.

'It happened this morning,' the Zookeeper began. 'There were so many visitors. We had all the usual school groups, of course, but there was also a busload of elderly guinea pigs from La Plata, a team of polo players and a delegation from Helsinki—'

'Goodness, what did they want?' asked Alberta, curiously.

'I never did find out,' replied the Zookeeper, 'as, alas, I speak no Finnish. In any case, I was extremely busy. I went to the Mongoose Mansion around lunchtime to make sure they had all had a good meal. And then I realised – our most prized mongoose was nowhere to be found. All that remains of him is this collar,' she added sorrowfully. 'I found it next to his bowl of brazil nuts.'

'Why is the mongoose so prized?' inquired Alberta.

'For his fluffy white tail, of course,' replied the Zookeeper, 'which, as you know, is not normal for mongooses.'

'Is that so?' said Alberta who, despite her large brain, did not actually know what was normal for mongooses.

'When did you last see him?' asked Coco.

'Let me think.' The Zookeeper strained to remember. 'I may have seen something running down to Rhino Ranch straight after morning tea, but really I can't be sure.'

'Are not the animals kept in cages?' asked Alberta, noticing with some alarm a large lion that seemed to be coming their way.

'This is a free zoo,' said the Zookeeper in a surprised voice. 'The animals are free to wander around as they please. It is our policy. The only exception is the Cats' Cradle,

where we do insist our newborn kittens stay in bed. In fact, we have just welcomed a most valuable litter of leopards.'

'It seems to me,' said Alberta, 'that your missing mongoose has probably been eaten by one of the other – er – carnivorous animals.'

The Zookeeper looked horrified. 'I can assure you, none of our animals would dream of doing such a thing!' she exclaimed. 'It is against our policy!'

'They may not need to dream of it,' suggested Alberta, 'they might just actually do it.'

She was relieved to see the lion turn a corner and disappear from sight.

'Please, Alberta, you're upsetting her,' muttered Coco. In a louder voice he said, 'Señorita, I think the little mongoose is probably just hiding somewhere. You know how playful these creatures can be.'

'I suppose it's possible,' said the Zookeeper, sounding unconvinced. 'You don't think it's more likely to be a case of kidnapping? There has been so much in the news lately about such things.'

'Let's not think the worst first, señorita,' said Coco, turning pale under his fur, as he did not at all like the sound of that. 'What we must now do is conduct a thorough search of the grounds, calling out the mongoose's name. That's sure to – er – ferret him out.'

'What a splendid idea!' said the Zookeeper, standing up. 'You are so clever,

Señor Coco. Now I must leave you. There's a television reporter waiting to interview me for the afternoon news. Good luck!'

And she took off at a rapid pace through a flock of flamingos, her lovely rainbow fur glinting in the sunlight.

'What a fine person!' sighed Coco, watching her go. 'So committed to mongooses.'

'Yes, yes, marvellous,' said Alberta, a little

impatiently. 'Now, about your plan, primo. It's excellent, but there's just one problem.'

'What's that?' said Coco, stepping out of his dream.

'We don't know the mongoose's name,' said Alberta. 'So how can we call it out?'

'Oh dear,' said Coco. But then he brightened. 'Wait a minute – what about the collar? Perhaps his name is marked on it.'

He picked the collar up and inspected it carefully. Sure enough, there along the inside edge was a row of little letters.

ENGOMOI'SOMA

There was a silence.

'I wonder how it is pronounced?' said Coco eventually.

Alberta's brain thumped. PING!

'Wait a minute, Coco,' she said. 'Look – each of the letters is fixed to the collar with glue. I think the letters must have fallen off and someone has simply stuck them back on without looking at the order they go in.'

'You mean—'

'I mean, this is not the mongoose's name, just the letters of it. If we rearrange the letters, we'll find his real name.'

'I don't know, Alberta,' said Coco, frowning. 'The Zookeeper would surely have

told us if something like that had happened. I mean…' He paused. 'ENGOMOI'SOMA is probably quite a common name in – um – wherever mongooses come from. I think if we roam the Zoo calling it out, the little mongoose is sure to come running.'

Alberta sighed. She did not believe for a moment that the mongoose's name was ENGOMOI'SOMA but she could see that Coco was hopelessly captivated by the glamorous Zookeeper. There was little she could do but agree to the plan.

WHAT DO YOU THINK?
CAN YOU MIX THE LETTERS
AROUND AND WORK OUT HOW
THE MONGOOSE'S COLLAR
SHOULD READ?

If you need help, turn to the back of the book.

Chapter Four

'ENGOMOI'SOMA! ENGOMOI'-SOMA!' shouted Coco.

'ENGOMOI'SOMA!' hollered Alberta.

The two guinea pigs scurried along the twisting pathways of the Zoo, from the Penguin Pond to the Lion Lodge, past the Gorilla Grange, the Vulture Villa and the Cockatoo Castle.

In keeping with Zoo policy, most of the animals were not in their expected homes. It was a peculiar experience to peer into the Kangaroo Korner and see a camel deep in conversation with a giraffe. But in every place, the animals lifted their heads and gazed solemnly, silently wishing Alberta and Coco good luck in their quest for the little mongoose.

'ENGOMOI'SOMA!'
'ENGOMOI'SOMA!'

On they went, past the Alligator Alhambra and the Tiger Taj Mahal, which was occupied by a family of white rabbits. Past the Cats' Cradle with its sign *'Shh! Nursing Mothers'* but not a cat or kitten in sight.

'ENGOMOI'SOMA!'

Past the Elephant Estate, the Dromedary Domicile and the Hippo Haven. The hippos, who were sunning themselves in the pool by the Panda Palace, raised three cheers for the Chief of Police – 'Hip-hippo-ray!' – which Coco found very touching.

But there was not a single sound or sight of the missing mongoose.

'I don't understand,' said Coco, mystified. 'Where could Engomoi'soma be?'

In Alberta's opinion, the mongoose was currently in the stomach of a large toothy animal. But she merely said:

'We haven't tried the Nocturnal Nook yet.'

Coco shuddered. The Nocturnal Nook was a special enclosure for animals that only came out at night. There were no windows, and only a small door leading in or out. Coco had never been inside it – he had never had the courage. Who knew what might happen to a guinea pig in there?

'Um, is it far away?' he asked in a quavering voice.

'No,' said Alberta. 'Actually, it's right here.'

Indeed it was. The forbidding, spiky building, which looked like several triangles that had fallen on top of each other, was directly in front of them, casting a long shadow.

'It is fate!' croaked Coco bravely. 'We must go in and seek Engomoi'soma!'

He pushed open the swinging door of the Nocturnal Nook and felt his way in, Alberta right beside him. It was so dark they could see nothing at all, let alone a mongoose. But they felt night creatures moving around them, the fluttering of wings, the scratching of dirt, short shallow breaths.

Neither of them wanted to call out the mongoose's name. What if there was some unseen owl with a curved beak and cruel claw nearby, ready to dive and pounce?

'I hope the Zookeeper is right,' thought Alberta, 'that none of the animals would dream of doing anything against the policy.'

They both stiffened. From somewhere deep in the darkness, they could hear whispered voices. They stood still as statues and listened.

'*Sew weave court thee kit ends. Wadder wee doon ow?*' said the first voice.

'*Weaken high dam inn sighed won ov thee Ann knee Mal play says four a why lentil nigh thyme,*' came the reply.

'*Hmm. Witch won? Theirs oh men knee.*'

'*Um, eye dough no. Yew gotten knee eye deers?*'

'Eye no! Thatch imp pansy play sin them idyll! It spur fact.'

'Write. Grate. Eye yule fall oh ewe. Let scat ow toff hear!'

The whispering stopped. There was a scrabbling sound of feet moving quickly, as well as a kind of dragging, as though something was being pulled along the ground. The swing door flapped open and closed again.

'Alberta,' said Coco, trembling. 'What on earth was that?'

'I don't know,' replied Alberta. 'But whatever it was, I think my brain could think about it much better outside!'

And the two guinea pigs clambered out of the Nocturnal Nook as fast as they could, back into the bright daylight.

CAN YOU WORK OUT WHAT THE WHISPERING VOICES WERE SAYING?

You will find some hints at the back of the book.

Chapter Five

Once they were safely outside, Coco and Alberta crouched for a moment in the shade of a huge bush covered with white flowers, waiting for their heartbeats to slow down. Alberta was just about to ask Coco what he intended to do next, when she felt something slap against her shoulder.

'Che!'

'What is it, prima?' asked Coco, startled. 'What's wrong?'

'It's very strange, Coco,' said Alberta, slowly, 'but I think that flower just hit me.'

She pointed to the middle of the bush, where a long, fluffy white flower was flapping about in the air. It moved, as though it was about to slap Alberta again.

She leaned forward and grabbed it, giving it a yank.

'Great carrots, Alberta!' said Coco, in astonishment. 'That's not a flower—'

'It's a tail!' declared Alberta, pulling it right out of the bush.

It was a tail! A thick, fluffy white tail. And at the end of the tail something else emerged from the green depths of the leaves.

There stood the missing mongoose.

'Engomoi'soma! We've found you at last!'

Coco threw his arms around the little lost creature in delight.

'Qué raro!' said Alberta. 'What on earth was it doing in there?'

The mongoose squirmed out of Coco's embrace, his eyes glinting and alert.

'Euyouweuuuuuu!' came the sound of a long, drawn-out yawn.

The bush moved again. Now something else was pushing its way out of the green thickness. Not something. Someone. A small brown, black and white guinea pig, with a face that was annoyingly familiar.

'Hello,' said the little guinea pig, brushing the leaves and loose blossoms from his fur.

'Vos! Otra vez!' spluttered Coco in disbelief.

Ernesto! That same supremely irritating little guinea pig who seemed to be at the bottom of every mystery they were called in to solve!

'What are you doing here?' said Alberta, when she found her voice.

'Me?' said Ernesto. 'I was at a trip to the Zoo with my kindergarten.' He sneezed. 'But then I got lost!' And his eyes began to fill with tears at the memory.

'Yes, well, you're found now,' growled Coco, because he knew what Ernesto was like once he started crying. 'But what were you doing hiding in the bushes with the missing mongoose?'

'Um, let me think,' said Ernesto, scratching his head. 'Well, we looked at some monkeys, that's right, and then we looked at some bears, and then we stopped for morning tea, that's right, and we sat down on the grass, that's right, and then I was just about to eat the special churros that my abuela always packs for me. That's my favourite and—'

'Get to the point!' barked Coco.

'I was about to eat it,' continued Ernesto in a wounded voice, 'when this mean little mongoose with a white tail hopped over, grabbed it, and ran away. So I ran after him. And he ran and I ran and he ran and I ran and he ran and I ran and he ran and I ran and—'

'Yes, yes, we understand,' said Alberta. 'Then what happened?'

'We came to a hill and the mongoose was a little bit slow and I was a little bit fast and I grabbed his tail. And he screeched and he scratched and I was about to get my churros back when I heard the chimes of the clock, you see,' said Ernesto. 'It was eleven o'clock, ding-dong, ding-dong, ding-dong, ding-dong—'

'Please!' said Coco. 'My head! It was eleven o'clock, so what?'

'Eleven o'clock is my nap time, of course,'

replied Ernesto, as though it was obvious. 'I always have my nap then. So I lay down under this bush for a nice little sleep. But I didn't let go of that mongoose, no way. I hung on tight. So now I am awake,' he finished, 'I would like my churros, please.'

Ernesto looked around expectantly. Unfortunately there was no sign of the churros, except perhaps a few grains of sugar on the smug lower lip of the no-longer-missing mongoose…

'Never mind that now,' said Alberta. We must get you back to your kindergarten teacher. She will be so worried about you!'

'Yes, well, much more importantly,' said Coco, who had managed to slip the collar over the neck of the white-tailed mongoose before he could get away again, 'we must tell the Zookeeper of our success!'

Suddenly the air was thick with a chopping noise and flying leaves. Alberta raised her claw to shield her face.

'I THINK YOU'LL BE ABLE TO TELL HER RIGHT AWAY, COCO,' she shouted. 'SHE'S COMING DOWN IN THAT HELICOPTER!'

Coco turned in amazement. There was the Zookeeper, in all her spectacular beauty, hopping out of a helicopter that had just landed next to the Chimpanzee Chateau. She was surrounded by television cameras and a variety of wild animals who were interested to see what was going on. The blades of the helicopter slowed down, and the noise dropped.

'Señor Coco!' said the Zookeeper in excitement. 'We spotted you from the search-and-rescue helicopter. You found him! You found Velma!'

She rushed over and covered the mongoose with kisses.

'Did you say Velma?' said Coco, taken aback.

'Isn't Velma a girl's name?' asked Alberta.

'Not amongst mongooses,' replied the Zookeeper, tickling Velma under his chin.

'Surely everyone knows that.'

'So what is the meaning of Engomoi-soma?' asked Coco, bewildered. 'The word on the inside of the collar?'

'Oh, that!' The Zookeeper smiled, her head to one side. 'I'm afraid the letters fell off somehow and got stuck back on again in a hurry, all mixed up. They should say "I'm a mongoose". It's just to remind him, you know – he does get confused at times.'

'I want my churros!' demanded Ernesto, very definitely.

'Aren't you gorgeous?' said the Zookeeper, smiling sweetly down and patting Ernesto's head. 'You must be the little boy I've had all the phone calls about. Your teacher and your abuela are wondering where you got to!'

Coco was about to inform the Zookeeper that Ernesto was in fact not gorgeous at all, when he noticed a pair of guinea pigs in dark purple hats at the entrance of the Chimpanzee Chateau, each carrying a large purple sack.

'I thought you closed the Zoo to the public?' he said to the Zookeeper with a frown, gesturing at the purple strangers. 'Who are they?'

The Zookeeper glanced up at where he was pointing.

'Oh, that is the delegation from Helsinki,' she explained. 'They are only in the city for one day, so I allowed them to stay. Perhaps I shouldn't have, but now we've got our mongoose back, there's no harm done.'

'Ha!' replied Coco. 'Don't be so sure!'

He had suddenly remembered something from his days in the Police Academy, about the strange language he'd overheard in the Nocturnal Nook. He plunged towards the purple-hatted pair.

They dropped their sacks in shock, and tried to bolt, but it was too late. Coco held them tight, one in each claw.

'I arrest you both for kidnapping,' Coco cried, 'in the name of the glorious police force of Buenos Aires!'

Chapter Six

Coco had done it again! He had captured the heartless kitten kidnappers, masquerading as members of the Helsinki delegation. Inside those purple sacks were

60

helpless leopard kittens, snatched from their nursing mothers in the Cats' Cradle, to be sold on the international market for outrageous sums of money.

The President declared a day's public holiday and there were fiestas and fireworks lasting long into the night. A State dinner was held in the Casa Rosada and the President herself pinned yet another shiny medal on Coco's red sash.

Naturally Alberta attended the ceremony, and they had a marvellous evening of fine lettuce and fountains of iced water. They danced till the sun rose.

'You must be so proud, Coco,' said Alberta as they sat resting after a particularly active tango. 'Look at that medal!'

'Yes, although they still seem to be having problems spelling my name,' said Coco. 'I wonder why they find it so difficult?'

'Ah well, Coco,' said Alberta, who also found it difficult, 'good spelling is not as important as a good heart, is it?'

'Claro, of course you're right, prima,' said Coco. 'Now, I was thinking, perhaps tomorrow we could go to the waterfalls at Iguazú for a picnic—'

'I'm so sorry, Coco,' said Alberta, 'but I cannot stay tomorrow. In fact, I'd better get going as soon as possible. I have a picture at home that needs hanging.'

Coco looked glum. Alberta was always rushing away.

'But you will come back, won't you?' he said, his voice filled with hope.

'Of course, primo, as soon as there is another emergency,' replied Alberta. 'You know where to find me. But now I'd best be off.'

And with that she picked up her brown-paper bag and scurried into the moonlight, down the long avenue, away from the palace.

It was a pity, thought Coco, watching her go, that his cousin lived so far away. For himself, he knew he could never leave Buenos Aires. He sighed and went and stood on the plaza outside the Casa Rosada, staying there until the sun rose high in the sky, humming the ever-comforting words of his favourite tango ...

My beloved Buenos Aires,
When I call your name,
Sorrow leaves my heart ...

CAN YOU CORRECT THE SPELLING OF COCO'S NAME?

CLUES FOR PUZZLES

IT ALL ADDS UP

This is an addition puzzle. There are a lot of numbers but it's not hard. You will work it out by trying different combinations of numbers to add up.

One combination is:

$$19+$$
$$72$$
$$88$$
$$94$$
$$\overline{}$$
$$273$$

I wonder if those are the buses Coco and Alberta took? But there are other solutions. How many more bus combinations you can find?

ANAGRAMS

An anagram is when you take all the letters in a word and mix them up to see if you can find another word or words.

For example, if you mix up the letters of *ALBERTA* you can get the words *REAL BAT* or even *ABLE RAT*. (Hmm, I don't think she'd like either of those!)

So in this puzzle, you just need to mix up all those letters on the collar of the mongoose to find out what it should say.

Here's a hint: it makes three words – and don't forget the apostrophe.

After you've worked it out, why not try mixing the letters of your own name around, and see what you come up with?

MONDEGREENS

The weird whispering voices are speaking in something called 'mondegreens'. This is when you hear a word, and you think it is another word that sounds the same but can mean something completely different!

The word 'mondegreen' comes from a poem:

'*They have slain the Earl of Murray, and they laid him on the green.*'

If you heard this out loud you might think it says:

'*They have slain the Earl of Murray, and the Lady Mondegreen.*'

A simple way to work out the guinea-pig mondegreen conversation is to read it aloud to yourself or another person. What do the words sound like?

For example, when the guinea pig says, 'eye no', it sounds like he doesn't want any eyes on his dinner plate.

But say it out loud.
'EYE NO!'
Now do you know?

NUMBER NAMES

This is a very strange zoo – instead of using words, all the animals are identified by numbers. The first number is the name, and the second number is the kind of animal.

I wonder if you can help Coco and Alberta crack the code and write the animal's name on the right collar?

351073 the 5181

318808 the 338

3773516 the 35006

312217 the 733

Hint: Try turning the page upside down. Look – the 3 becomes an E. What letters do the other numbers turn into? Aha!

Can you write Ollie the Egg in the same way?

GLOSSARY

abuela (ah-bway-lah) grandmother

a ver (ah vair) let's see

Casa Rosada (cah-sa rose-ah-dah) the Pink House, the palace of the President of Argentina

che! (chay) hey!

churros (choo-ross) a kind of long doughnut

claro (clah-roh) sure, of course

empanada (em-pah-nah-dah) a little meat pie

Iguazú (ig-wah-soo) a place of giant waterfalls on the border of Argentina and Brazil

otra vez (oh-trah vess) again

prima (pree-mah) girl cousin

primo (pree-mah) boy cousin

qué raro! (kay rah-roh) how strange!

señor (sen-yor) Mr or sir

señorita (sen-yor-eet-ah) Miss

vamos! (bah-moss) let's go!

vos (voss) you

zoologico (zoh-oh-lo-hee-coh) zoo

CHURROS!!

HELP COCO (AND ALBERTA

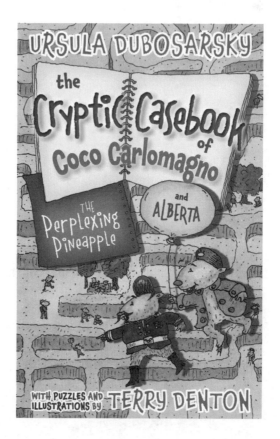

Every afternoon from his office high in the
Obelisco, Coco sees a floating pineapple and
hears a terrible sound. Is he being haunted?

CRACK MORE CASES!

From his office high in the Obelisco, Coco
has intercepted a mysterious message that
could only mean one thing – or could it?